SHIP
OF THE
DEAD

Titles in Dark Reads:

Badger Publishing Limited, Oldmedow Road, Hardwick Industrial Estate, King's Lynn PE30 4JJ
Telephone: 01438 791037

www.badgerlearning.co.uk

SHIP OF THE DEAD

ALEX WOOLF

Shp of the Dead ISBN 978-1-78464-087-3

Text © Alex Woolf 2015
Complete work © Badger Publishing Limited 2015

Publisher: Susan Ross
Senior Editor: Danny Pearson
Publishing Assistant: Claire Morgan
Copyeditor: Cheryl Lanyon
Designer: Bigtop Design Ltd
Illustrator: Aleksandar Sotirovski

2 4 6 8 10 9 7 5 3 1

Printed by Bell and Bain Ltd, Glasgow

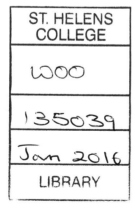

CHAPTER 1
SEASICK

Zac was feeling seasick. "I so wish I hadn't come on this cruise," he groaned.

"Then you'd never have met me and Seth," pointed out Callie.

"You couldn't ask for better friends than us," said Seth. "After all, we skipped dinner last night to keep you company!"

"Yeah, thanks for that," muttered Zac.

"I could murder some breakfast," said Seth.

They set off for the dining room.

"Where is everyone this morning?" Callie wondered. "The ship seems deserted."

Suddenly, a crewman appeared. He began lurching towards them.

"Excuse me, where is everybody?" Callie asked the crewman.

He didn't reply. He just kept stumbling towards them.

"There's something wrong with him," said Zac. "Look at his eyes."

"Hey, what are you doing?" Seth shouted as the man grabbed him.

"Watch out!" yelled Callie.

The man opened his jaws wide. Seth tried to break free but his grip was like iron.

Callie kicked the crewman hard in the ribs. He staggered backwards and fell overboard.

"You've killed him!" cried Seth.

"He looked dead already," said Zac.

CHAPTER 2

INFECTED

More people appeared. They had the same dead eyes as the crewman, the same lurching walk.

"They're coming towards us!" cried Seth.

The friends hid behind a lifeboat.

"What's going on?" gasped Callie.

"Something on last night's menu must have infected everyone," said Zac. "Lucky we missed dinner."

"The ship's turning in circles," Seth suddenly noticed. "No one's steering."

"We have to get to the bridge," said Callie. "Use the radio to signal for help."

They dashed from their hiding-place.

Zombie passengers and crew staggered towards them, teeth bared, arms outstretched.

"Here's the bridge," yelled Callie, pulling open a door.

As they entered, the dead captain seized Callie.

His teeth began to close around her neck. Seth dragged Callie out of the way but the captain bit him on the arm.

Seth screamed.

Zac grabbed a stick he found and stabbed it into the captain's head.

CHAPTER 3
SOS!

"SOS!" Callie cried into the radio. "This is the Aurora! Is anyone there?"

There was nothing but static.

Seth had passed out. Zac checked his pulse. "I think he's dying," he said. "We should throw him overboard. He might be infected."

"No!" shouted Callie. "He saved my life."

Seth's heart finally stopped beating.

Over the next hour, zombies tried again and again to break into the bridge.

Suddenly, Seth's eyes opened. Callie bit back a sob. Then she killed him in the only way that seemed to work with zombies – by smashing his head.

There was a loud ripping noise and the whole ship shuddered. Callie and Zac were thrown to the floor.

"We must have hit some rocks," groaned Zac. "We're sinking."

"We'll die if we stay in here," said Callie. "We have to get to that lifeboat!"

Callie and Zac struggled along the deck as waves crashed around them. They tried to fight off the zombies, but there were too many.

"We're not going to make it," panted Zac. "The lifeboat's too far."

"I'm not going to become one of them," whispered Callie.

CHAPTER 4

HELP!

Just then, a huge wave broke over them.
It washed the two friends right off the ship.

"Help!" cried Callie. She choked as her lungs
filled with sea water.

She was sure she was going to drown.
Then her hands found some driftwood.

The water was dark and cold.

Barely conscious, the friends clung onto the driftwood.

It seemed like hours later when they woke up on a deserted beach.

"What happened?" croaked Callie.

Zac looked at her and managed a smile. "We survived," he said.

STORY FACTS

THE ZOMBIE LEGEND

The legend of zombies began on the island of Haiti in the Caribbean. In Haitian folk tales there is a kind of black magic called Voodoo. People called bokors used Voodoo to bring people back from the dead and turn them into zombies. A zombie is a slave to the bokor and has no will of its own.

In the twentieth century, zombies became popular villains in books, films and comics.

George A Romero's film *Night of the Living Dead* (1968) introduced a new breed of zombie, hungry for human flesh.

QUESTIONS

Who was feeling seasick?
(page 5)

What had infected everyone on the ship?
(page 12)

Who was bitten by the captain?
(page 16)

What saved Callie and Zac from drowning?
(page 26)

Where did the legend of the zombies begin?
(page 30)

Who made the film *Night of the Living Dead*?
(page 30)

MEET THE AUTHOR

Alex Woolf is the author of over 80 books, mostly for children and young adults. He wrote a science-fiction trilogy called *Chronosphere*, and *Aldo Moon*, about a teenage Victorian ghosthunter. *Soul Shadows* is a horror story about flesh-eating shadows.

MEET THE ARTIST

Aleksandar Sotirovski is from Macedonia. He is an illustrator with over 25 years' experience. He has worked on lots of children's books, textbooks and posters. He is also a concept artist for comics and games.